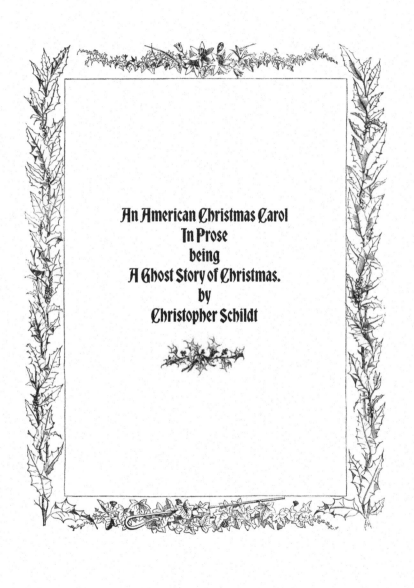

An American Christmas Carol
In Prose
being
A Ghost Story of Christmas.
by
Christopher Schildt

Print ISBN: 979-8-35095-099-1
eBook ISBN: 979-8-35095-100-4

First printing 2024

Printed in the U.S.A.

Based on

"A Christmas Carol"

by

Charles Dickens

Contents

BOSTON, 1843

Marley's Ghost

EDWARD MARLEY WAS DEAD—TO BEGIN with. There can be no doubt whatsoever about that. The certificate of his death had been signed by a clergyman, the chief undertaker, and the clerk of the Essex County Court of Massachusetts and filed at the State Hall of Records. With undeniable certainty, old Marley was as dead as a doornail!

Port Gloucester is where it ended for Marley. It was a coastal fishing town thirty miles east of Boston, where the salty mist from the sea could be smelled and tasted. There was an overbearing odor from low tide and dead fish, while overhead, the sky was filled with flocks of seagulls hovering in circles. Extending far from the shore was a long wooden dock that rocked and creaked with the incoming tide. That was where the fishing boats, which sold their catch at the Gloucester Fish Market, moored when not out to sea. It was there on the dock where Marley died while serving a notice of foreclosure at Christmas.

He slipped on the damp wood, fell, and struck his head. Marley rolled off the dock and into the murky waters, where he drowned.

Henry Rutherford knew that Marley had died. How could it be otherwise? The two had been partners in the law firm Marley & Rutherford for over fifty years. Rutherford had been Marley's only friend for as much as either of the two could know friendship, and Rutherford was Marley's only mourner. Still, Rutherford was not so terribly saddened by the news of Marley's death—only that he had lost an excellent litigator. That was the extent of Rutherford's sorrow over Marley's demise—but it was more than old Marley deserved.

It was the chief undertaker of Port Gloucester who delivered the news of Marley's death to Rutherford. Dressed in a black suit with tails, a black cravat, and a stovetop hat, the undertaker was a grim sight to behold. The man was old, tall, and thin, and his pointed nose was red at the tip. With his shoulders slouched, elbows bent, and his hands poised like a praying mantis, he stood before Rutherford at the law firm, which was in the cheapest district of Boston. Rutherford sat at his desk, staring intently at the papers he held. He never once raised his head to look at the undertaker, even upon hearing the news of Marley's death.

After the undertaker declared old Marley dead, Rutherford wasn't the least bit interested in what the man had to say next. It was sufficient to know that his partner was dead; to Rutherford's way of thinking, there was nothing else to discuss. He gave the undertaker just enough money to bury old Marley in Port Gloucester, where he died. Marley was buried there to spare the cost of transporting the old wretch back to the city. The coffin would be made of pine because it was cheaper that way. The headstone was equally cheap, with only Marley's name and date of death crudely chiseled into a rough piece of field-stone. Rutherford told the undertaker to choose a burial plot. It didn't matter to Rutherford, or anyone else, what part of the graveyard Marley would be planted in, since no one would come to visit. Rutherford didn't care, as long as it was the least expensive spot in the graveyard. And with payment to the undertaker made in full, old Marley was truly gone—forever. Soon, it was as if he'd never even existed.

Rutherford had never painted over Marley's name on the sign at the law firm after he died. So, there it hung for years outside the front door of their dingy redbrick office: Marley & Rutherford. It was not to pay tribute to Marley through some form of grief—because there was none. It was a well-established fact that Rutherford didn't care about Marley, but he *did* care about the cost of a sign maker and a bucket of paint. It was simply cheaper to leave the sign the way it was and save money. From the very beginning, the law firm was known as Marley & Rutherford. People who were new to the office would get the two lawyers confused. In reality, there was no difference between Marley and Rutherford. In terms of their greed and malevolence, the two were actually the same. No better than Marley was Rutherford. And no better than Rutherford was Marley. In that respect, the sign was still quite accurate.

Everything about Henry Rutherford was as dark and cold as a grave. A tight-fisted hand at the grindstone—a greedy, wheezing, grasping, scrapping old sinner—was he. No freezing wind that ever blew so fiercely in winter was more bitterly cold than Henry Rutherford. He had an icy gaze, a soul as dark as a shadow blending seamlessly with the night, and a wrinkled face frozen with a nasty sneer, warning the world around him to keep their distance.

Rutherford never engaged in any form of conversation unless it had to do with money, nor did he ever exchange any pleasantries with those he encountered around Boston. When he was forced to speak, Rutherford would deliver an answer in a manner that was quick, sharp, and angry, and his expression sour. To his way of thinking, idle conversation was a waste of his time, and for old Rutherford, time was money.

In the taverns of Boston, there was life and movement with the flux of the carefree common folks. They would arrive at the taverns to drink, toss a few darts, and dance to a fiddle with merriment. There was singing, joking, questions, and greetings. "Fine weather! Your health? Hello—goodbye." In the city taverns, there was happiness. But the whole idea of joy and life at the taverns was washed away by Rutherford's grim appearance each night when he came to eat his dinner. It was as if the sun was eclipsed, and the Earth fell into darkness the moment he stepped into the room.

Rutherford ate the scraps left on the plates of unfinished dinners, which were dumped in a large pot and sold as "seconds." It was cheaper that way, at just two pennies per meal. When he was finished, Rutherford would wipe his face on the sleeve of his old wool jacket before walking out of the room, eyes forward and with a menacing glare, serving as a warning to those who stood in his path to step aside.

Rutherford's house had once been a stately mansion—but no more. The walls were dark and dirty, with peeling, discolored wallpaper. The curtains were like torn rags draped over the windows. Every once in a while, the curtains would eerily drift back and forth as a bone-chilling wind seeped through the cracked panes of glass. Down a long hallway was the room where Rutherford sat every night by a wood-burning fireplace. It was the only room in the old estate that was illuminated, but only by the flames. For Rutherford, the fire served two purposes: to keep the room lit and warm. And it was in this dingy old room, by the fire, in a torn, dirty, high-winged chair, that Rutherford ate his slop out of a chipped soup bowl. He lived there all alone in that old mansion that looked like a haunted house.

This was the world that Rutherford had built for himself—brick by brick—over the past sixty years. Angry and bitter were but two words that, through his own choices in life, truly defined his existence. No! There was nothing about Henry Rutherford that would leave an impression—other than to say that he was a very horrible man.

* * *

It was now Christmas Eve, and seven years after Marley's death. As kindness, goodwill, and charity were celebrated in all their festive glory there in the city and around the world, Rutherford sat working at his desk at the law firm. Outside his office, it was snowing steadily, and had done so for most of the day. The sidewalks and streets of the city were covered in freshly fallen snow. A parade of horse-drawn carriages would clip-clop down the cobblestone street, leaving behind their tracks until more snow would cover the street again, leaving no trace of the traffic that had come before; likewise, for the footsteps of the people walking on the sidewalk. The crowds of cheerful city folks traveling down the streets were as festive as the season, bidding one another a "Merry Christmas."

By Rutherford's window, an old man with a violin played songs of the holiday for spare change, which was gladly donated out of appreciation for the joy of the music that he so cheerfully played. Near to him was a vendor selling roasted chestnuts from a smoking pot, which was considered an excellent tummy warmer on such a snowy day.

Except for Rutherford glaring and shaking his fist in anger at the cheerful crowd of smiling faces through his office window, annoyed at the activities outside, everything truly was a splendid example of Christmas, even for the cheap side of the old city. The snow, the Christmas music, the roasting chestnuts, and the cheer of the people—it truly was perfect! It was this sort of perfection of the holiday, and the happiness it brought, that Rutherford truly hated.

"Merry Christmas, Uncle!" Rutherford heard a cheerful woman's voice loudly exclaim from the small lobby by his office. It was Julia Wickham, Rutherford's young niece and, most importantly, his only surviving family member.

Rutherford pretended not to hear her, but Julia knew otherwise.

"I say it again, Uncle… Merry Christmas!" said Julia even more loudly than before. She was now standing at his office door, making her greeting impossible to ignore. Still, Rutherford was silent.

"I say it for a third time, Uncle, and I shall keep saying it until I hear it back." Julia giggled. "Merry, merry, merry Christmas, you old poop!"

That's the way it was between Julia and Rutherford. She annoyed him, and she did so intentionally. It gave her a silly sense of pleasure to see and hear the old grump complain, but she truly meant him no harm.

"Christmas? Nonsense!" answered Rutherford sharply.

"You can't possibly mean that."

"I do, and with every fiber of my being!" said Rutherford, glaring at her angrily. "It's nonsense. Complete foolishness. And you're a fool for thinking otherwise!"

This was a dispute that Rutherford and Julia had every Christmas. It was a scene that replayed itself each year during the holidays. It had become something of a tradition—a ritual between the two—and if not for the dispute, there would be nothing at all to do with Christmas for Rutherford.

"You can't truly believe that," said Julia. "There must be something resembling a warm feeling in you—somewhere deep down inside your stinky old clothes!" 6

"Nothing! How could it be otherwise? I live in a world of fools, niece! Merry Christmas? Humbug, I say! What is it, but for a time to find yourself another year older and not a penny richer or wiser? If it were up to me, every fool walking around with 'Merry Christmas' on his lips would be tarred, feathered, and dispatched into the wilderness tied to a donkey!"

Julia couldn't help laughing at such nonsense.

"It's not meant to be funny!" shouted Rutherford. "It's true! Christmas is the practice of foolishness. It is without meaning, except for the foolish! And what right do *you* have to be merry, huh? You're homely, and because of it, you have no husband and no children. Never will either! You'll be an old spinster living all alone, except for a house full of dirty cats. And you're frail and poor! So, what cause have you to be happy at this or any other time of the year?"

"Don't be nasty, Uncle. I am beautiful where it counts. Inside me, there's nothing but beauty," said Julia. "I am, and I shall always be, merry at this and every other time of the year."

It was true. Julia *was* beautiful, and her greatest attribute was her smile. Everything Julia ever did, she did it with a gentle smile. She was sincere and walked at eye level with the rest of the world. Everything about her was pure and loving. Yes, indeed! Julia truly was beautiful.

"Why do you insist on wasting my valuable time?" Rutherford yelled. "Each year, you invite me to dinner, and each year, I turn you down. What will it take to send you away and stop this nonsense about Christmas?"

"Dine with me for Christmas, Uncle. You're the only family I have left. Come! Please! It's what my mother would have wanted. Be with me. No one should be alone at Christmas."

"Goodbye, niece! There's nothing more to be said. Go!"

"Uncle, please… I want nothing from you other than your love. And maybe—possibly—for you to be proud of me. You're all that I have for family."

"If I'm all that you have, then consider yourself all alone in the world," said Rutherford—cold and cruel. "There's nothing for you here. Go away, you ugly spinster!"

"Very well, Uncle. But eventually, it will come to be… for Mother's sake. We *will* celebrate Christmas together, and we will be a family," said Julia with warmth and compassion. Julia always showed him far more compassion than Rutherford deserved, and certainly far more than he would show others, despite the tragedy of their circumstances. "Should you change your mind—"

"I won't!" Rutherford quickly interrupted, slamming his fist against the top of his desk. "Go!"

Julia did as he commanded. She left him alone in his office without a word spoken in anger because she had no such feelings toward him. On her way out the door, she said "Merry Christmas" to Rutherford's clerk, William Cratchit. He was a most pleasant man who had been employed by the firm for over ten years. Cratchit was thin and well-worn by the harsh life he had lived, particularly under the grindstone of Marley and Rutherford. He was more of a scarecrow than an average man and was always nervous—mostly to do with his employers.

Cratchit sat at his desk in a gloomy, freezing area of the building. There was no heat to speak of for him—only a single burning piece of coal in a fireplace near his desk. As commanded by Rutherford, Cratchit could burn only a single piece of coal, which is why he kept himself huddled under a blanket at his desk and did his best to warm the tips of his fingers above the flame of a candle while he worked. For

8

Rutherford, Cratchit was little more than a plow horse to be whipped and beaten in the fields. Employment was scarce in the city, and with a wife and five children to support, Cratchit took the terrible abuse. He had no other choice, even with such a meager salary, which was barely enough to keep his family housed and fed.

"A Merry Christmas to you as well, Miss Julia," Cratchit returned cheerfully.

After a most pleasant exchange with Cratchit, Julia left the firm. Soon after, the hour arrived for work to conclude for the day. Cratchit closed his ledger and was quick to extinguish his candle to be certain that no more wax would be wasted on light than absolutely necessary. That's how Rutherford wanted it to be. Like time, the wax of a burning candle was money. The only remaining light near Cratchit came from Rutherford's office. Cratchit adjusted his top hat and wound his scarf around his neck, the winter chill seeping through the office windows. He was about to leave when he heard Rutherford calling out his name.

"You'll be wanting the whole day off tomorrow, I suppose," Rutherford said, his face as sour as ever, still seated at his desk.

"If it's convenient, Mr. Rutherford," Cratchit replied, his voice timid.

"It's not!" Rutherford snapped, his tone sharp with anger. "I shouldn't have to pay a full day's wages for no work. What do you say to that?"

"Christmas comes but once a year, sir," Cratchit said cautiously, "and it's more for my family than for me."

Rutherford glared at Cratchit in silence for a moment that seemed to stretch into eternity. Finally, he relented. "Very well, take the day. But be here earlier the next morning. If not, you may seek employment elsewhere!"

Cratchit nodded, his gaze fixed on the floor, and quickly left the room, avoiding Rutherford's sneer and display of absolute discontent.

Once Cratchit was gone, two dignified gentlemen entered Rutherford's office. They were impeccably dressed in tailed waistcoats, high-collared shirts, and perfectly tied cravats, their top hats adding an air of confidence to their appearance. These portly gentlemen, pleasant to behold, greeted Rutherford with a bow, books and papers in hand.

"Marley and Rutherford, I believe," said one of the gentlemen, referring to his list. "Have I the pleasure of addressing Mr. Rutherford or Mr. Marley?"

"Mr. Marley is dead!" Rutherford replied. "He died seven years ago this very night. Now, as my time is valuable, what do you want?"

"At this festive season of the year, Mr. Rutherford," said the gentleman, taking a pen from his pocket, "it is necessary to make provisions for the poor and destitute, who suffer greatly. Thousands are in desperate need of common necessities, such as food and warm clothing."

Rutherford bristled at that. "Are there no prisons or insane asylums?"

"Plenty," said the gentleman.

"And the workhouses?" demanded Rutherford. "Are they still in operation?"

"They are," returned the gentleman, "though I wish I could say they were not."

"The sweat factories and labor camps, then?" asked Rutherford.

"Both very busy, Sir."

"Oh! Excellent! I was afraid, from what you said, that something had occurred to stop them in their useful purpose," said Rutherford. "I'm very glad to hear it."

"A few of us, Mr. Rutherford, are endeavoring to raise money to buy the poor food and means of warmth. We choose Christmas because it is a time, of all others, when want is keenly felt, especially among the children. What shall I put you down for?"

"Nothing!" Rutherford replied.

"You wish to be anonymous?"

"I wish to be left alone!" Rutherford slammed a fist against his desk. "Since you ask me what I wish, gentlemen, that is my answer. I don't celebrate Christmas myself, and I can't afford to make idle people merry. I help to support the establishments I have mentioned through taxes. They cost enough, and those who are badly off must go there!"

"Many can't go there, and many would rather die."

"If they would rather die," said Rutherford, "they had better do it and decrease the surplus population."

"But you must understand the need?" observed the gentleman.

"It's not my business!" Rutherford returned, his tone sharp and cutting. "It's enough for a man to understand his own business and not to interfere with other people's. My business occupies me constantly. Good afternoon, gentlemen!"

Seeing clearly that it would be useless to pursue their point, the pair quietly withdrew from his office. Rutherford continued with his work, feeling quite proud—and he laughed, amused by the idea that he could care about anyone other than himself.

* * *

It was completely dark outside when Rutherford finished work for the day on that Christmas Eve. Everyone was gone, and he was all alone as he walked down the empty city streets that led to his dreary old estate. It was still snowing fairly heavily—not that it mattered to Rutherford. The darkness, cold, and snow had no effect on him other than to cause him to occasionally brush the white powder off his shoulders where it had collected.

When he reached the black iron gates of the old mansion, a wintery, thick fog enshrouded the place, making it difficult to see. Rutherford had walked that very long stone path from the gates to his front door for almost fifty years. Even so, he fumbled through the darkness. Once through the front door, Rutherford double-locked himself in, as was his custom.

Rutherford performed his nightly ritual of lighting the fire, preparing his meal, and then settling into his ragged chair by the hearth with his chipped soup bowl, with what amounted to slop cradled in his lap. For most of the meal, everything was silent and predictable, except for the occasional crack and pop of the burning wood and the clink of his spoon striking the sides of the bowl as he ate.

Rutherford happened to glance at an unused, rusted servant's bell mounted over the entryway. Without explanation, the bell began to sway back and forth, as if moved by a strong wind. Suddenly, the bell stopped moving and began to ring loudly. The piercing ring played on Rutherford like the sound of shattering glass. It became so loud that he was forced to cover his ears; if he did not, the sound would cause him physical pain. Through it all, the bell never moved. Then, all the servant's bells throughout the old mansion started to ring in unison, and the sound was deafening. It all lasted no more than a few minutes, but for Rutherford, it felt like hours, and when it finally stopped, it left him terribly shaken.

The silence, now that the bells had stopped ringing, was short-lived. It was quickly replaced by the clanking of metal striking the marble floor of the grand hall below, as if heavy steel chains were being shaken and dragged across its smooth surface. The sound of the dragging chains grew louder by the moment, echoing throughout the old, dark mansion. Rutherford could now hear them being pulled up the long, ornate staircase, accompanied by the clomp-clomp-clomp-clomp of footsteps on its wooden treads approaching the door of the room in which he sat. A moment of silence passed before the door burst open with so much force that it was nearly torn from the hinges. A white mist seeped into the room, chased by the foul odor of a murky low tide. Moving through the mist was a bluish figure that looked like a man walking toward the fireplace. Rutherford felt a chilling mix of fear and fascination, his skin prickling with the ghostly touch of a cold, unearthly presence.

As this phantom drifted closer to Rutherford, he could see it more clearly, but not as clearly as he would see any mortal man standing before him. Other than different shades of blue and purple, the phantom was somewhat transparent. Rutherford could vaguely see the room through what should have been a solid body. Its features were clear enough for Rutherford to see the clothes it was wearing with a large degree of detail—but not a face. He could see a waistcoat, tights, cravat, and boots. The phantom was wrapped in thick chains attached to a heavy iron money safe, which, like the apparition itself, was transparent. It looked like it had just stepped in from the pouring rain with the way its clothes were drenched, and it was covered in seaweed, as if the phantom had crawled out of the ocean.

Any reasonable person would have been terrified by these events—particularly by the appearance of this phantom—but not Rutherford! He was far too cold and arrogant to have such feelings, even in the presence of a ghostly apparition. Rutherford looked at the phantom with a nasty expression, and with a tone of defiance and anger, he asked, "Who are you?"

The phantom moved slightly closer but still kept a respectable distance. "Ask me who I *was*."

"Very well. Who *were* you?"

The phantom walked closer to Rutherford, dragging the heavy chains and iron safe. "In life, I was your law partner—Edward Marley."

Now that the phantom stood close to Rutherford, he could see his face clearly. There was no mistake, particularly with the distinctive pigtail, long nose, and voice. It certainly did look like Edward Marley, and Rutherford felt a brief chill as his dead-cold eyes stared down at him. Still, it was difficult to believe—that there he stood before him— the ghost of Marley.

"Humbug!" Rutherford exclaimed.

"Do you believe in me?" the ghost inquired.

"I don't!" said Rutherford defiantly. "Edward Marley is dead and gone!"

"What evidence would you have of my reality beyond your senses?"

"I don't know."

"Why do you doubt your senses?"

"Because," said Rutherford, "many things affect them. A slight disorder of the stomach. You may be an undigested bit of beef, a crumb of cheese, or a fragment of an undercooked potato. There's more of gravy than of grave about you—whatever you are!"

At this, the ghost released a spine-chilling cry and shook his chains wildly. Suddenly, and without reasonable explanation, there was a blinding flash of lightning through the window, chased by a howling wind and a deafening clap of thunder that rattled the room.

"Man of the worldly mind!" shouted the ghost. "Do you believe in me or not?"

"I do! I must. But why do you haunt me? What do you want?" asked Rutherford, caustic as ever.

"Everyone has a purpose that must be fulfilled," said the ghost. "If not in this life, then in the next. Until then, there can be no rest— not even, as for me, at the bottom of the ocean, weighed down by these chains."

The ghost emitted a pitiful shriek and rattled its chains again with shadowy hands.

"I don't understand," said Rutherford. "You speak in riddles. And why the ocean? You were buried quite properly and at great expense to me, I might add. Nothing but the finest for you, dear friend. I gave you rest in a beautiful plot underneath a weeping willow to symbolize my sorrow at your loss. And the finest of coffins. Oh! It truly was magnificent! Mahogany, with polished brass handles and lined with ivory silk imported from the Orient. The tombstone was Italian polished marble. I spared no expense for you, dear Edward."

"No!" said the ghost, who released a long, pitiful sigh. "But no less than I deserved as such a miserable wretch. Dropped into the ocean, I was, and so bitter to the taste that not even the sharks would have at my body. Oh, woe is me! Now I cannot rest. I cannot linger anywhere. My spirit is doomed to wander the Earth in agony. It is a perpetual nightmare."

"And what of this purpose that must be fulfilled? Revenge?" asked Rutherford. "If it is revenge you seek for what has been done to you, then revenge you shall have! There *will* be terrible consequences for this crime." Rutherford stood with his fists clenched so tight that his knuckles turned white. "The undertaker and his lot will be imprisoned for the remainder of their miserable lives. I will file a lawsuit against them. I will take everything they own, and their families will live in the gutter, eating from a garbage can. This, I vow to you, dear friend."

"No!" answered the ghost ruefully.

"Then what? Speak plainly to me. What do you want?" Rutherford shouted angrily.

"It is required of every man that the spirit within him should walk abroad among his fellow men and travel far and wide with compassion. That is our purpose! But if that spirit goes not forth in life, it is condemned to do so after death. It is doomed to wander the world and witness what it cannot share but might have shared on earth and turned to happiness." The ghost let out a piercing cry, shaking and clanking its chains wildly. "Oh, not to know the ages of struggle by mortal creatures, for this earth must pass into eternity before the good to which it is susceptible is all developed. Not to know that any good spirit working kindly in its little place, wherever it may be, will find its mortal life too short for its vast means of usefulness. Not to know that no space of regret can make amends for one's life's opportunities misused! Yet, such was I! Oh, such was I!"

"But dear Edward, you were always a good man of business," faltered Rutherford, who began to apply this to himself.

"Business!" cried the ghost, rattling its chains again. "Mankind was my business. The common welfare was my business; charity, mercy, kindness, and benevolence were all my business. The practice of law and the dealings of my trade were but a single drop of water in the vast ocean of what was my business!"

The ghost held up the money safe at arm's length, as if that were the cause of all its horrible grief, and threw it heavily upon the floor.

"Why did I walk through the crowds of fellow beings with my eyes turned down and never raise them for a moment to see the sorrow and suffering of others?"

Rutherford made no reply. He tried to speak some words of comfort but had none to offer the ghost.

"I am here tonight, this Christmas Eve, to warn you that you have a chance of escaping my fate. A chance and hope of salvation," said the ghost. "You will be haunted by three spirits."

"If that's the chance you speak of, then I decline," said Rutherford. "I'd rather not."

"Without their visits," said the ghost, "you cannot hope to escape the path I have traveled. Expect the first when the bell strikes one. Expect the second when the bell strikes two, and the last when the bell strikes three."

The ghost slowly drifted backward from Rutherford. With the sound of the heavy money safe and chains dragging across the wooden floor, the ghost continued on its path back toward the door through which it had entered.

"Look to me no more, Henry. And may God have mercy on your soul," said the ghost. Soon, it vanished from sight. The door slammed shut when it was gone, and the mist quickly followed, leaving the room as it was before its appearance. Rutherford hesitantly glanced to his right and then to his left. There was nothing!

The strange event had ended, and all was silent, leaving Rutherford to question the reality of what had transpired. Marley's ghost bothered him, and every time he resolved himself that it was all just a hallucination, his mind replayed the events, leaving him to ask, *Was it a dream or not?*

The First of the Three Spirits

Aﬔﬔﬔ CAREFUL CONSIDERATION, RUTHERFORD DECIDED to give the ordeal no more thought. He climbed into his bed and covered himself with heavy layers of blankets to counter the freezing temperature of the room. Quickly, he fell asleep, but was awakened by a hand shaking his shoulder vigorously. Rutherford heard a young woman's voice say, "Henry, wake up! Wake up!"

The room where he slept was no different from any other in the old estate. It was dark and cold, with the only light provided by a single candle in a brass holder on a small table next to his bed. Despite this meager light, the room remained gloomy. But it was different at this moment. Rutherford turned his head toward the voice, and as soon as his eyes opened, he was blinded by a brilliant light. The room was so bright that he had to shield his eyes with his hand.

Once his eyes became adjusted, he could see a very young woman standing next to his bed. A majestic green robe, the color of fresh holly leaves and trimmed in gold, draped gracefully around her shoulders, and reached down to the floor. Atop her head was a crown of holly, red berries, and gold-and-silver ribbons. The high-collared shirt she wore was a fanciful red velvet trimmed in silver. She had flowing black hair, her skin a fine white porcelain, rosy cheeks tinged with the freshness of youth, and large, round, crystal blue eyes that sparkled. Unlike Marley's, her body appeared mortal. Her smile was broad, and everything about her demeanor was cheerful and innocent.

In her tiny hand, she held a magnificently crafted golden torch embellished with intricate engravings of holly and cherubs. Its flames, which burned brightly in hues of yellow and orange while emitting the pleasant scent of fresh-cut pine, were the source of illumination that had so blinded Rutherford. No king's scepter could be grander than this torch. It spoke of the ages.

"Are you the spirit whose coming was foretold to me?" asked Rutherford. He sat up in his bed, his thinking still clouded because he had just been awakened from a profound sleep.

"I am!" answered the ghost gleefully, with a smile so broad that it plumped her rosy cheeks and made her eyes twinkle.

"Who, and what, are you?" Rutherford demanded.

"I am the Ghost of Christmas Past," she announced with a high degree of pride, and with that, she bowed her head graciously.

"Long past?"

"No! *Your* past," answered the ghost.

She held out her hand as she spoke and clasped Rutherford gently by the arm. "Arise, Henry, and walk with me!"

Her grasp, though gentle, could not be resisted. Rutherford could have argued that the weather and late hour were detrimental to his well-being, that his bed was warm, that the thermometer had dropped well below freezing, and that he was dressed in only his sleeping gown and nightcap. But he rose from his bed without protest. The ghost walked him to a window, which was magically opened by the mere passing wave of the beautiful torch she held.

"May I remind you that I am mortal and shall fall to my death, unless that is the manner of my demise, and this be the moment of my death," said Rutherford.

"Keep hold of my hand," answered the ghost, "and you shall be upheld and safe from harm."

As her words were spoken, they passed through the window, and then mysteriously, Rutherford and the ghost now stood on a country road with crisp air, a blue sky, evergreens lush with wintry beauty, and snow-covered fields that glistened like fine crystal under the morning sun. Though it was winter where they stood, it was warm to Rutherford. The cold had no effect on him or the ghost. The old city of Boston had vanished, replaced by nature that wasn't the least bit affected by the thoughtless touch and greed of man.

"Good Heavens!" said Rutherford. With a sense of joy, he clasped his old, wrinkled hands. "I know this place. I was here as a child."

The sight and smell of the surroundings had a profound effect on Rutherford, and each sensation brought back warm, joyful memories and feelings that he had long since forgotten. It caused him to smile, which in itself was an impressive accomplishment for such a hardened old sinner. The ghost looked at Rutherford and smiled warmly, appearing quite pleased with herself at what she had achieved—causing Rutherford to smile with such delight.

"You remember this place?" asked the ghost.

"Remember it?" Rutherford smiled with a sense of childlike delight. "I could walk this path blindfolded!"

"Strange that you could have forgotten so much of what appears to have made you so happy—once," observed the ghost. "Let us walk closer, Henry."

Rutherford and the ghost walked the long road, and along the way, he remembered everything as they moved toward a small snow-covered New England town in the distance. They crossed a bridge that led them toward a schoolhouse that rested by a winding river. Horses, with young children laughing joyfully on their backs, trotted toward them. The young ones were in great spirits, singing and shouting at each other until the surrounding fields were filled with the music of wonderful, innocent children at play. They were happy, and Rutherford was truly elated to see what was transpiring before them.

"These are but shadows of things long past," said the ghost. "They cannot see or hear us, Henry. To them, *we* are the ghosts!"

This merry group of children on horseback traveled forward, and as they came, Rutherford knew and named each of them to the ghost. But why should such a bitter old wretch, such as Rutherford, rejoice beyond all bounds to see these children? Why did his eyes glisten and his heart leap as they went past? Why was he filled with such joy when he heard them bid each other a merry Christmas as they parted at crossroads and byways for their respective homes? What was Christmas to Rutherford? Christmas? Oh! What good had it ever done for him?

"The school is not quite deserted," said the ghost. "A solitary child neglected by his friends and family is left there still."

Rutherford knew it and resisted the urge to weep.

Rutherford and the ghost left the road by a well-remembered lane and soon approached a schoolhouse of dull red brick. On the roof was a cupola with a bell hanging in it. Despite its size, the building was in terrible disorder. The walls were damp and musty, the windows broken, and the gates rusted and decayed. The stables and the coach house were terribly neglected, overrun with tall weeds. From an enormous set of double doors, Rutherford and the ghost entered the dreary, musty hall and, glancing through the open doors of many rooms, found them poorly furnished, bleak, and barren.

They walked across the hall to a door at the back of the schoolhouse. It opened before them, revealing a long, bare, melancholy room made even barer still by rows of empty wooden desks. At one of these, a lonely boy read a book near a meager fire. It was Rutherford as a child—his poor, forgotten self as he used to be. He nearly wept at the sight of the lonely boy.

The building was as silent as a graveyard, except for a whispering wind that carried through from the broken panes of glass in the arched windows. Not a voice, not an echo, not a squeak or scuffle from the mice behind the walls, not a drip from the half-thawed waterspout in the dull yard behind, not the idle swinging of doors—no, not a crackling of flames in the fire. There was nothing but horrible silence.

In pity for his former self, Rutherford said, "Poor child!" and struggled to keep his tears at bay. "I wish," Rutherford muttered, "but it's too late now."

"What is the matter?" asked the ghost.

"Nothing," Rutherford answered in a whisper.

"Something, I believe," said the ghost.

"There was a boy singing a Christmas Carol at my office last night. Dirty. Sickly. Ragged. All alone. Oh! Dear sweet child. I should have given him something, that's all."

The ghost took Rutherford by the hand, and her touch was gentle. She held up the torch, which burned brightly, though less so than a moment ago, and waved it in the air, saying, "Let us see another Christmas!"

* * *

Rutherford's former self was now a young man, and the room at the old schoolhouse had become a little darker and dirtier. The panels had shrunk, the windows had cracked, and fragments of plaster had fallen from the ceiling. The vision before them was quite correct, as everything had happened just as it appeared: there he was—older but alone again, as all the other boys had gone home for Christmas.

His younger self wasn't reading now, but walking up and down the halls of the old school building in despair. Rutherford looked at the ghost, mournfully shaking his head, and then glanced anxiously toward the front door. He knew what was to come next.

The schoolhouse door swung open, and a little girl, much younger than himself as a boy, came darting in excitedly. The child, wearing a pink bonnet, had curly blonde hair, rosy cheeks, and a smile as bright as the morning sun. She put her arms around his waist, and addressed him as "Dear, dear brother."

"I've come to bring you home, dear brother!" said the child joyfully, clapping her tiny hands and bending down to laugh. "To bring you home—home at last, brother!"

"Home, Amanda?" he asked.

"Yes!" said the child, brimful of glee. "Home for good. Home forever and ever. Father is so much kinder than he used to be that home is like Heaven! He spoke so gently to me one dear night when I was going to bed that I was not afraid to ask him once more if you might come home. And he said *yes*, you should, and sent me in a coach to take you home. And you're to be a man!" said the child, opening her twinkling eyes wide. "And you are never to come back here. But first, we're to be together all Christmas long and have the merriest time in all the world."

"You're quite a woman, little Amanda!" exclaimed the boy.

She clapped her hands, laughed, and tried to touch his head, but being too little, she only laughed again and stood on tiptoe to embrace him. Then, she dragged him by the hand, in her childish eagerness, toward the door. Desperately wanting to go, young Rutherford followed.

A dreadful voice in the hall cried out, "Bring down Master Rutherford's trunk at once!" In the hall appeared the wicked old schoolmaster himself, who glared at Rutherford with ferocious disdain. The horrible abuse young Rutherford had suffered over the years in this awful place was finally over—thanks to little Amanda, who had come to his rescue.

Young Rutherford's trunk was tied to the top of the carriage, and the horse galloped onward, down the long country road, and away from this terrible place. Soon, it was gone from the wicked schoolmaster's sight.

"Always a delicate creature, whom a breath might have withered," said the ghost. "But she had a large heart!"

"She did. You're right. I won't deny it!"

"Amanda died a woman," said the ghost, "and had, as I remember, a child."

"One child," Rutherford answered.

"Your niece—Julia!"

Rutherford seemed uneasy and answered quietly, "Yes."

"Julia is of her body. Love her as you did, Amanda."

Rutherford covered his face with his hands and wept. He responded with a nod.

"Come, Henry," said the ghost. "There's more to see."

* * *

The ghost waved her torch again, and they were now in the busy thoroughfares of a city. It was clear to see, by the dressing of the shops trimmed in garland and pine wreaths with red bows, that here, too, it was Christmastime again. But it was evening, and the streets were lit up. A warm glow emanated from the gas streetlamps that lined the cobblestone paths, casting a glow on the snowy landscape. As the ghost and Rutherford stood on one of the paths, shadowy figures, shadowy carts, and shadowy coaches passed them by like phantoms.

The ghost stopped at a large warehouse with tall brick walls and rows of windows, and the air outside the building was filled with the smell of burning coal. The ghost asked Rutherford whether he knew the place.

"Know it?!" said Rutherford. "I was a clerk here."

The ghost and Rutherford went inside. At the sight of an old gentleman sitting behind a high desk, Rutherford said with great excitement, "Why, it's old Mister Fezziwig! Bless his heart. It's Fezziwig alive again!"

Old Fezziwig laid down his fountain pen on his ledger and looked up at the wall-mounted clock, whose hand pointed to the hour of seven. He rubbed his hands together briskly, adjusted his waistcoat, laughed, and called out in a jovial voice, "Henry! Edward!"

Rutherford's former self, now grown into a young man, came quickly, accompanied by his fellow clerk, Edward Marley.

"My dear boys!" said Fezziwig. "No more work tonight. It's Christmas Eve, Edward! Christmas, Henry! Shutter up the windows," old Fezziwig cried out, laughing merrily.

Young Rutherford and Marley excitedly charged out to the street to shutter the windows and then ran back inside.

"Clear away everything, my lads, and let's have lots of room here! Edward! Henry! Clear it all away!"

Everything that could be moved was packed off, the floor swept and washed, the lamps trimmed, fuel heaped upon the fire. That winter's night, the old warehouse was snug, warm, and dry.

In came a fiddler with a music book, and he went up to Fezziwig's desk, using it as a platform on which to perform. In came old Mrs. Fezziwig, along with her daughters, beaming and lovable, followed by the six young suitors, whose hearts they broke. In came all the young men and women employed in the business, in came Fezziwig's housemaid with her children and the baker, and in came the cook and the milkman. In they all came, one after another: some shyly, some boldly, some gracefully, some awkwardly, some pushing, some pulling. In they all came.

Old Fezziwig cried out, "Well done, my lads!"

There were dances—waltzes, ballroom promenades, and more. Spread out across rows of tables were cake, a magnificent roast beef, apple and cherry pies, and plenty of beer. But the great effect of the evening came after the roast and desserts, when the fiddler struck up "The Wassailing Song" of Christmas, and old Fezziwig danced with Misses Fezziwig. Soon, all the partygoers joined them in a dance. The ladies, with their flowing gowns, together with the men, twirled gracefully to the cheerful melodies played on the fiddle, spreading the festive spirit of Christmas throughout the room. As the dancers glided across the wooden floor, laughter and joy filled the air, and with this, old Fezziwig smiled with delight.

When the clock struck midnight, the festivities ended. Mister and Misses Fezziwig took their stations, one on each side of the door, shaking hands with every person individually as he or she went out and wishing them a Merry Christmas.

"A small matter," said the ghost, "to make these silly folks so full of gratitude."

"Small?!" echoed Rutherford.

"Why? What he spent on this celebration was meager—three or four dollars, perhaps. Does he truly deserve such appreciation?"

"It's not that," said Rutherford, heated by the remark. "It isn't that at all. Fezziwig, as our employer, had the power to render us happy or unhappy… to make our work light or burdensome, a pleasure or a toil. He chose to make us happy, and that happiness he gave was as great as if it cost a million."

Rutherford felt the ghost's glance and stopped.

"What is the matter?" asked the ghost.

"Nothing."

"Something, I think?" the ghost insisted.

"No," said Rutherford. "I would have liked to say a word or two to my own clerk just now. That's all."

Rutherford looked at the scene, which was slowly fading into darkness. He watched Fezziwig standing before his younger self and a younger Marley. He placed something in the palms of their hands and said, "Thank you. Thank you both for all your hard work. Merry Christmas, lads. I am as proud of you as any father could be of a son."

"What was that he placed in your hands?" inquired the ghost.

"Three gold coins each—for both of us," Rutherford answered. A tear trickled down his wrinkled cheek. "Marley and I used those six gold coins to open our law firm after our graduation."

"The same firm today?" asked the ghost. "Same place?"

"The very same," Rutherford replied quietly. "And we prospered!"

"Indeed!" the ghost agreed. "And now Edward Marley is the richest man at the bottom of the ocean."

To this, Rutherford said nothing.

The flame of the grand torch held by the ghost was slowly fading and was now burning in hues of bluish purple. "My time grows short," observed the ghost. "We must be quick!"

* * *

The ghost waved the torch, and now they were standing in a park, with the sun casting its golden light over the wintry landscape. Families and friends were gathered by a frozen pond, ice skating. The sound of laughter and joyful chatter filled the air as skaters glided gracefully across the mirror-like surface of the pond. The aroma of warm cinnamon and spiced apple cider filled the air as snowflakes fell gently, adding to the enchantment of the scene. It was all so beautiful, which was wasted on the likes of Rutherford but not on the ghost, who stood cheerfully watching these festive activities.

Again, Rutherford saw himself. He was older now—a man in the prime of life. An eager look in his eyes showed the hunger for wealth and power that had taken root. He was not alone, but rather sat on a wooden bench by the pond at the side of a fair young woman in a flowing overcoat. The woman was crying. It was Rebecca, who had once been Rutherford's fiancée.

Rebecca was a very attractive young woman with features as gentle and pure as the freshly fallen snow. She looked like a ballet dancer, with her brown hair kept in a bun, beautiful emerald eyes, and thin physique, and she moved with a gentle grace, like a feather drifting through the air. The gown she wore was simple—not overstated—and this was the way she wanted to be seen by others.

"I now understand," she said to Rutherford's younger self, "that another idol has replaced me, and if it can cheer and comfort you in time to come, as I would have tried to do, I have no just cause to grieve."

"What idol has displaced you?" asked Rutherford.

"A golden one."

"This is how it is with the world!" said Rutherford. "There's nothing noble about poverty, and there is no greater cause than the pursuit of fortune! Wealth is power! The law is power!"

"You see the world as you want it to be," she answered gently. "I have seen your nobler aspirations fall off one by one until a master passion—wealth and power—engrosses you. Have I not?"

"I've grown so much wiser in the way of the world," Rutherford replied. "But my feelings for you haven't changed."

She shook her head ruefully. "Our pledge of love is an old one. It was made when we were both poor and content to be so until, in good time, we could improve our fortune by honest labor. You *have* changed. I've seen you in courtrooms corrupting the truth with your lies to serve your own means. In doing so, you've corrupted the law."

"Truth is subjective," Rutherford said defiantly.

"A lie is a lie!" she retorted. "You've become a different man."

"I was just a naive boy when we met," Rutherford said impatiently. "I knew nothing about the world."

She removed her engagement ring from her finger and placed it in his hand. "I release you, Henry, from your promise of marriage. With a full heart, for the love of the man you once were, may you be happy in the life you've chosen. Goodbye, Henry!"

She left him, and that was the last time he saw Rebecca.

"Spirit," said Rutherford, "show me no more! Take me home. I've seen enough!"

"One shadow more!" replied the ghost.

"No more!" exclaimed Rutherford angrily. "I don't want to see it. Show me no more!"

But the ghost grabbed him by the arm and forced him to observe what happened next.

And with one last wave of the grand torch, she transported them to another scene and place. It was a room in a modest home—not very large or handsome, but full of warmth and comfort. By a crackling winter fire sat a beautiful young girl who looked so much like Rebecca that Rutherford believed it was her, until he saw Rebecca, now much older but just as beautiful, sitting opposite the young girl.

"Rebecca's daughter," said the ghost. "Such a beautiful young woman. One of the three children she had."

"She could have been mine," said Rutherford solemnly. "I could have been a father."

Just as he said this, a distinguished gentleman entered the room. It was Rebecca's husband, and now Rutherford looked on more attentively than ever as the gentleman sat down with her and the child at the fireside.

"Rebecca," said the husband, turning to his wife with a warm smile. "I saw an old friend of yours this afternoon."

"Who was it?"

"Guess!"

"How can I?" she answered, laughing as he laughed.

"It was Henry Rutherford. When I passed his office window at the law firm, he had a candle burning at his desk. His partner has died, I hear, and there he sat alone. Quite alone in the world, I do believe, and at Christmas, no less."

"Spirit, remove me from this place at once!" said Rutherford in a broken voice.

"I told you these were shadows of the things that have been," said the ghost. "That they are what they are. Do not blame me!"

"Remove me!" Rutherford hollered. "I cannot bear it! Take me back! Haunt me no longer!"

Rutherford forced the torch from the ghost's hand and smashed it on the frozen ground, causing the last of the dying flame to be extinguished. And when this happened, everything went dark as night.

There was nothing!

STAVE III

The Second of the Three Spirits

WITH A GASP, RUTHERFORD AWOKE in his bed, his heart pounding against his chest. Beads of sweat glistened on his forehead, and with trembling hands, he reached for a match to strike a flame to the candle by his bed, desperate to chase away the shadows of what had transpired moments ago with the visit of the Ghost of Christmas Past. As a circle of light illuminated his bed, Rutherford took a deep breath, grounding himself in familiar surroundings.

The grandfather clock in the corner of the dark room chimed once and then twice. *Expect the second ghost when the bell strikes two,* Rutherford thought. He got up, slid into his slippers, and shuffled away from the bed. At that moment, he heard a strange voice call out his name, followed by a burst of light from underneath his chamber door—so bright that it might be the middle of the day. But Rutherford knew otherwise.

Rutherford walked to his chamber door, hesitantly turned the doorknob, and entered the adjoining sitting room. It was indeed his own, but it had undergone an amazing transformation. The room

33

exuded the essence of Christmas in all its grandeur and elegance. The air carried the inviting warmth of a flame that was suddenly burning in the fireplace, casting a soft, golden hue upon the room. Garland, holly wreaths with red bows, and mistletoe adorned the walls.

Every corner of the room was filled with delightful aromas, an array of delectable treats and desserts beckoning from ornate tables and sideboards. Rutherford had never seen anything like it before—certainly not at the old estate. It was glorious!

"Come in!" exclaimed the ghost. "Come in! And know me better, man!"

Rutherford timidly entered and hung his head before the next ghost.

"I am the Ghost of Christmas Present," said the ghost, smiling joyfully. "Look upon me!"

Rutherford did so. Perched atop a towering golden throne was a dark-skinned jolly giant of what looked like any mortal man with a heavy black beard. Its brown eyes sparkled, and its voice was cheery. It was clothed in one simple green robe bordered with white fur. The garment hung so loosely on the figure that its large breast was bare. Its feet, observable beneath the folds of the garment, were also bare, and on its head, it wore a holly wreath set here and there with shining icicles. In its left hand was the same grand torch carried by the Ghost of Christmas Past, but burning even brighter than before—and twice the size—were its yellow flames.

"You have never seen the likes of me before!" exclaimed the Spirit.

"Never," Rutherford answered.

"Have you never walked forth with the younger members of my family?" asked the ghost.

"I don't think I have," said Rutherford. "Have you many brothers, Spirit?"

"Over eighteen hundred," said the ghost.

"A tremendous family to provide for," Rutherford muttered.

The Ghost of Christmas Present rose.

"Spirit," said Rutherford. "Conduct me where you will."

"Touch my robe!" said the ghost, releasing a hearty laugh. "We have much to see."

Rutherford did as he was told and held it tight in his quivering hand as the ghost waved the torch. As he did so, everything joyful in the sitting room instantly vanished, returning to its cold and dreary state; quickly, the room itself also disappeared.

* * *

The ghost and Rutherford now stood in the bustling cobblestone streets of Boston as a busy Christmas day was unfolding. It was daylight, and the air was crisp; the snow-covered city lay wrapped in festive decorations. People rushed their way through the crowded streets, filled with excitement and holiday cheer. The aroma of roasted chestnuts and freshly baked gingerbread wafted through the air, drawing people toward the lively market square. Vendors stood proudly behind their stalls, displaying their wares with great enthusiasm. Colorful scarves, handmade toys, and shiny trinkets caught the eyes of the cheery folks who passed by the shops.

As they strolled down the city street, the ghost and Rutherford paused by a group of common folks gathered around a chestnut vendor, warming their hands on the steaming bags. Laughter filled the air as they shared stories and exchanged playful banter. The vendor, with a twinkle in his eye, listened to their jovial conversations, occasionally joining in with his own humorous remarks.

"They seem to be happy?" Rutherford said, as if there was something peculiar about happiness. It was strange to him that these people should find so much joy in something as simple as a steaming pot. "Have they never seen chestnuts cooking?"

"It's not that," said the ghost, laughing.

"I don't understand."

"Perhaps you will soon enough," replied the ghost. "Come!"

They walked farther down the street and stood watching a flower vendor skillfully arrange bouquets of vibrant red poinsettias. A gentleman approached her stall.

"These flowers will make my wife so happy," he confided with a smile.

The vendor added a few extra blooms to the bouquet at no extra charge, wishing him a "Merry Christmas."

"Imagine that…" said the ghost. "Placing happiness above profit."

Rutherford said nothing, but felt a sense of shame.

The ghost waved the torch, and now they were in another district of Boston—one where few would dare travel, certainly not the likes of Rutherford. It was the poorest section of the city, but despite the poverty, it emanated a spirit of joy for the holiday. The people, especially the children, found solace in the celebration of Christmas. Amid the biting cold, families gathered in their modest homes, their meager feasts reflecting the challenges they faced. The flickering candlelight cast a soft glow on a table with deep cuts down the middle, illuminating scanty, smudged faces filled with anticipation.

Outside, the snowflakes danced from the gray sky, covering the streets and rooftops with a pristine white blanket as a bitter wind whispered through the narrow alleyways. The children, with rosy cheeks and tattered clothes, ventured into the streets, their voices rising above the snow-laden silence. Their harmonious melodies filled the air as they sang Christmas carols with unabashed enthusiasm. Passersby paused to listen to the sweet tunes that resonated through the frosty air.

Rutherford and the ghost witnessed great acts of kindness there in the poorest district. Neighbors shared what little they had, and the Salvation Army extended a helping hand to those in need: a warm cup of soup, used clothing, a comforting smile, and a heartfelt conversation became gifts far more valuable than gold or silver.

Witnessing so much kindness toward the poor made the ghost smile.

* * *

The ghost led Rutherford straight to his clerk's house. Through a window, they watched Mrs. Cratchit, William's wife, who was dressed modestly in a secondhand gown but adorned with a holiday ribbon, set the table with the help of their daughter, Belinda. Their son, Peter Cratchit, cheerfully helped by cooking the potatoes for their dinner.

The Cratchits' two younger children, a boy and a girl, burst in, screaming that they had smelled the goose cooking outside the baker's shop and knew it was theirs. Excitedly thinking about the delicious sage and onion stuffing, the children danced around the table, praising Peter while he stoked the fire in the oven until the potatoes boiled and banged on the pot lid, begging to be peeled.

"What's keeping your father?" Mrs. Cratchit asked. "Your brother, Tim? And where's Martha? She wasn't this late last Christmas day, not even by half an hour."

"Here she is, Mother," said Peter, as Martha stepped into the kitchen.

"Here's Martha!" the two young Cratchits cried out. "Hooray! Martha, you won't believe the goose we have!"

"Well, my dear, you're finally here," Mrs. Cratchit exclaimed, kissing Martha and taking off her shawl and bonnet for her.

"We had a lot of work to finish up last night at the factory," Martha replied, "and had to clean up this morning, Mother."

"Well, never mind. As long as you're here," Mrs. Cratchit said. "Sit by the fire, my dear, and warm yourself. God bless you."

"Father is coming!" the two young Cratchits shouted, running around in excitement. "Hide, Martha, hide!"

So, Martha hid, and William Cratchit, carrying Tiny Tim on his shoulder, came in with at least three feet of scarf hanging in front of him, along with his patched and brushed-up clothes to look presentable for the occasion. Tiny Tim relied on a little crutch and had his withered legs supported by a metal brace. William had been carrying Tim all the way from church.

"Where's Martha?" William asked, looking around.

"She's not here," Mrs. Cratchit replied. "She's not coming!"

William's spirits suddenly dropped. "Not coming on Christmas Day?"

Martha didn't want to see him disappointed, even if it was just a joke, so she came out from behind the kitchen door and ran into his arms, while the two young Cratchits carried Tiny Tim over to a pot cooking pudding on the stove, so he could watch it bubbling.

"And how did little Tim behave in church?" Mrs. Cratchit asked.

"He was as good as gold," William replied. "Even better. Somehow, he gets very thoughtful when he's in church and thinks about the most extraordinary things. On the way home, he told me that he hoped people saw him in church because, being a cripple, it might give them pleasure to remember on Christmas Day how the Lord made disabled beggars walk and blind men see." William's voice cracked and trembled as he shared this, and it trembled even more when he mentioned that Tiny Tim was growing strong and healthy—but he knew otherwise. The child's health was deteriorating.

As they spoke, William rolled up his sleeves and prepared a hot drink with cider and lemons, stirring it round and round before placing it on the stove to simmer. Peter and the two young Cratchits went to fetch the goose, and quickly returned with it in grand excitement. And indeed, it was quite a joyful moment, as Mrs. Cratchit prepared the gravy in a sizzling hot sauce plate, as Peter vigorously mashed the potatoes. The little daughter sweetened the apple sauce with sprinkles of sugar, and Martha dusted the dinner plates.

The two young Cratchits set out chairs for everyone, and William sat Tiny Tim next to him in a small corner of the table.

Finally, the dishes were placed on the table, and grace was said. There was a moment of suspense as Mrs. Cratchit, slowly examining the carving knife, prepared to plunge it into the breast of the goose. And when she did, and the long-awaited burst of stuffing came pouring out, there was a chorus of delight from everyone at the table. Even Tiny Tim, inspired by the enthusiasm of the two young Cratchits, pounded the table with the handle of his knife and weakly cried, "Hooray!"

That goose was truly something special. William said he didn't believe a goose like that had ever been cooked before. Its tenderness, flavor, size, and affordability were all subjects of their admiration. With the addition of apple sauce and mashed potatoes, it was a wonderful meal for the whole family. In fact, as Mrs. Cratchit happily pointed out, while surveying a small speck of bone left on the serving plate, they had finished it all, but everyone had eaten enough.

Now, with the plates cleared, it was time for Mrs. Cratchit to leave the room to bring in the pudding. Suddenly, there was a lot of steam as the pudding was taken out of the copper pan. Mrs. Cratchit entered the room, flushed but proud, carrying the pudding. It looked like a speckled cannonball, hard and firm, with half a pint of ignited brandy blazing on top, adorned with a piece of Christmas holly.

"Oh, what a wonderful pudding it is!" William declared, with calm certainty, going on to say that it was the greatest success Mrs. Cratchit had achieved since their marriage.

Everyone had something to say about the pudding, but no one thought or said that it was too small for a large family. That would have been unthinkable. Any Cratchit would have been embarrassed to suggest such a thing; instead, they were grateful and felt blessed.

Finally, when the dinner was over, the tablecloth cleared, the hearth swept, and the fire replenished, it was time for the next part of the celebration. After tasting and approving the holiday punch, apples and oranges were placed on the table, and a shovel full of chestnuts was thrown into the fire. Then, the entire Cratchit family gathered around the hearth, forming a half-circle with the family's meager glassware. There were two tumblers and a custard cup without a handle. These vessels served their purpose just as well as golden goblets would have, and William cheerfully distributed the hot beverage while the chestnuts crackled and popped in the fire.

Then, William made a toast: "A Merry Christmas to all of us, my dears. God bless us."

The whole family echoed the sentiment.

"God bless us, everyone!" added Tiny Tim, the last to speak. He sat very close to his father, perched on his little stool. William held Tim's small, withered hand, wanting to keep him close by his side.

"Ghost," said Rutherford, with a newfound interest, "tell me if Tiny Tim will live."

"I see an empty seat in the poor corner of the chimney, and a crutch without an owner, carefully preserved," replied the ghost. "If nothing changes in the future, the child *will* die." The ghost glared at Rutherford. "But why should you care? If he's to die, then he should do so and decrease the surface population."

"You use my own words against me," uttered Rutherford.

"They're *your* words, not mine!" exclaimed the ghost. "Perhaps you should be more mindful of the surface population, and when you think of them, consider this tiny, sickly child."

Rutherford answered the ghost with his head lowered, and his voice was close to a whisper. "I shall!" said Rutherford. "May Heaven forgive me. I shall!"

There wasn't anything particularly impressive about this family. They weren't fanciful or well dressed. Their clothes were minimal. Despite all this, they were happy, grateful, and content with each other and the time they had together.

As they faded from view, their smiles lingered in the light of the ghost's torch, drawing Rutherford's gaze, especially to Tiny Tim, until they were no longer visible.

* * *

Nightfall descended, accompanied by heavy snowfall. Walking through the streets with the ghost, Rutherford marveled at the warm glows emanating from the fires in kitchens and living rooms. Inside the homes, families were busy preparing cozy dinners, with hot plates baking in front of the fire and curtains being drawn to shut out the cold and darkness.

Children dashed out into the snow to welcome their relatives, while guests gathered in some houses. Groups of girls, wearing hooded coats and fur boots, chatted as they visited nearby neighbors. Every home seemed to be expecting company, with fires burning brightly.

Suddenly, they found themselves in a desolate landscape strewn with huge stones, resembling the headstones of giants. Water flowed freely, except where it was frozen solid. Nothing but moss and coarse grass grew there. The setting sun cast a fiery red glow in the west, briefly illuminating the desolation before darkness engulfed it.

"Where are we?" asked Rutherford.

"This is where miners live who work deep underground," replied the ghost. "But they know me. Look!"

Approaching a hut with a glowing window, they found a cheerful group gathered around a warm fire. An old man and woman, their children, and grandchildren, all dressed in modest holiday clothes, were singing a Christmas song. The old man's voice, barely audible over the wind, grew livelier with each chorus.

The ghost didn't linger; it urged Rutherford to grasp its robe, and they floated above the moor toward the sea. Looking back, Rutherford saw a menacing range of rocks and heard the thunderous sound of the ocean crashing against the shore. On a lonely reef stood a solitary lighthouse, its base covered in clumps of seaweed, with seagulls circling overhead. Despite the desolation, two men watching the light had lit a fire, casting a warm glow through a loophole in the thick stone wall. They raised their glasses and wished each other a merry Christmas, while one, with a weather-beaten face reminiscent of an old ship's figurehead, sang a song of Christmas joy.

* * *

The ghost and Rutherford continued their ethereal flight above the black, heaving sea, tasting the salty mist as they soared with the sound of crashing waves below them. They flew until they reached a United States warship patrolling the coast to protect a nation, its silhouette stark against the horizon.

Now standing on the deck, they stood beside the helmsman at the wheel, feeling the rough, worn-smooth wood beneath their fingers, which had been touched by countless hands before theirs. The lookout in the bow peered into the darkness, alert for any sign of danger, the crisp sea air filling their lungs with each breath. The officers on watch whispered among themselves, their voices hushed yet filled with a camaraderie born of shared duty and purpose.

Around them, dark, ghostly figures moved, humming Christmas tunes that drifted like echoes from another world. They spoke of past Christmas Days spent at home, their words filled with longing and hope. Every sailor on board, whether awake or asleep in his hammock, had taken part in the festivities in his own way, whether by sharing a simple treat or a heartfelt story, while thinking of those they loved back home. They knew that their service at sea was keeping a nation safe from harm, and that thought filled their hearts with pride and determination.

The ghost, its gaze soft with admiration, spoke in a voice that seemed to blend with the sound of the sea. "Those who defend a nation," said the ghost, "Bless their courageous souls in Heaven."

* * *

With a wave of the grand torch, the ghost and Rutherford were now in Boston again. By this time, it was getting dark and snowing heavily as they walked along the cobblestone streets. Rutherford was overwhelmed with a sense of dread as he listened to the howling wind and contemplated what unknown horror might lie ahead. But suddenly, he heard a hearty laugh. It turned out to be his own niece's laughter, and Rutherford stood with the ghost in a bright and cheerful room in Julia's apartment. Nestled on a quiet street in the Roxbury district of Boston, her modest abode was adorned with the spirit of Christmas. The air was filled with the sweet aroma of freshly baked gingerbread and cinnamon as the sound of a crackling fire and joyful chatter echoed through its walls. There was a glowing Christmas tree decorated with delicate handmade ornaments and flickering candles by a humble feast spread across a old wooden table, including a steaming pot of mulled wine. Rutherford's niece laughed again. When she did, her dearest friend, Mary Schaffer, released a laugh of her own, and all of her friends, who had come to celebrate Christmas with Julia, quickly joined in.

"He said that Christmas was a humbug. Can you believe it?" exclaimed Julia. "And he actually believed it."

"Shame on him," said Mary, with indignation.

"He's quite a bitter old man," said Julia. "That's the truth. And he's not as pleasant as he could be. However, his own actions will be his punishment, and I have nothing against him."

"I'm sure he's very wealthy, Julia," hinted Mary.

"What does that matter, my dear?" replied Juia. "His wealth is of no use to him. He doesn't do any good with it. He doesn't even make himself comfortable. And he certainly doesn't have the satisfaction of thinking that he will ever benefit others with it."

"I have no patience for him," Mary observed. The other ladies at the Christmas celebration expressed the same sentiment.

"Oh, I have," said Julia. "I feel sorry for him. I couldn't be angry with him, even if I tried. Who suffers from his ill-temper? Only himself. He decides to dislike me for reasons I will never understand and refuses to join me for dinner. And what's the result? He misses out on a good meal."

"Actually, I think he's missing out on a *fantastic* meal!" Mary said. Everyone else quickly agreed, and they had every right to judge, having just finished a wonderful dinner and now gathered around the fire, with dessert on the table as the lamplights cast a warm glow.

"I was going to say," said Julia, "that if he dislikes me and refuses to celebrate with us, the consequence is simply that he misses out on pleasant moments that wouldn't harm him in any way. I'm certain he's missing out on better company than he can find in his dreary old office or dusty mansion. I intend to offer him the same opportunity every year, whether he likes it or not, because I feel sorry for him. He may complain about Christmas until the day he dies, but he can't help but think better of it—I challenge him. If he sees me going there year after year with a good attitude, saying 'Uncle Rutherford, merry Christmas,' maybe it will inspire him to be kinder toward others, and that would be wonderful. And I have to say, I gave him quite a shake yesterday."

Now, it was Julia's guest's turn to laugh at the thought of Rutherford shaking. But being good-natured and not caring much about what they laughed at, as long as they were laughing, Julia certainly didn't mind.

After tea, they enjoyed some music. Julia played the harp, and among other tunes, she played a simple little melody so easy that you could whistle it in two minutes, which had been familiar to Rutherford when he was a child and was reminded of by the Ghost of Christmas Past. When the music played, all the memories of the things the Ghost of Christmas Past had shown him flooded his mind. He softened even more, and thought that if he had been able to listen to such music years ago, he might have learned to be kind and happy without resorting to the cold loneliness that sent Edward Marley to the bottom of the ocean.

But they didn't spend the whole evening on music. After a while, they played games because it's good to be childlike sometimes, especially at Christmas. First, they played a game of blind man's buff. Of course, they did, and the way Julia moved around, trying to catch someone, was quite amusing. It was all good fun, and everyone laughed.

Mary did not join in the game of blind man's buff at the party. Instead, she settled herself comfortably in a large chair and footstool, tucked away in a snug corner where the ghost and Rutherford lingered close behind. However, she did join in the game of forfeits.

The ghost was delighted to find Rutherford in such a cheerful mood and regarded him with such favor that Rutherford, like a boy, begged to be allowed to stay until the guests departed. But the ghost said that could not be done.

"They're playing a new game," Rutherford pleaded. "Just a bit longer—please."

It was a game called Yes and No. Mary had to think of something, and the rest had to guess what it was. The rapid-fire questioning to which Mary was subjected revealed that she was thinking of an animal—a live animal, rather disagreeable, savage, sometimes growling and grunting, sometimes talking, roaming the streets of Boston, not exhibited anywhere, not led by anyone, not in a zoo, and not a horse, donkey, cow, bull, tiger, dog, pig, cat, or bear.

Mary burst into laughter each time a new question was posed.

Finally, Julia exclaimed, "I've got it! I know what it is, Mary! I know!"

"What is it?" Mary asked.

"It's my Uncle Rutherford!" And indeed, it was.

While some argued that the answer to "Is it a bear?" should have been "Yes," since a negative answer would have diverted their thoughts from Mr. Rutherford, assuming they had any thoughts in that direction, everyone was impressed by Julia's deduction.

"He has given us plenty of amusement," Julia said, "and it would be ungrateful not to toast to his health. Here's a glass of mulled wine, ready for us all, and I say, 'To Uncle Rutherford!'"

"Well! To Uncle Rutherford!" they all cried.

"A Merry Christmas and a Happy New Year to the old man, whatever he is," said Mary. "He wouldn't accept it from Julia, but may he have it anyway. To Uncle Rutherford!"

Rutherford had become lighthearted without the ghost noticing. He would have raised a glass to the company and thanked them if the ghost had given him time. But the whole scene ended as soon as his niece spoke the last word, and he and the ghost were on the move again.

* * *

The ghost and Rutherford embarked on a journey that took them to countless places, each ending in a scene of profound happiness. In hospitals, they stood by the beds of the sick, witnessing patients who, despite their ailments, radiated cheerfulness. They ventured into foreign lands where the unfamiliar became welcoming and familiar. Among the impoverished, they found resilience and patience, a steadfast hope for a brighter tomorrow. Among the poor, they discovered richness in the bonds of family and friendship. Wherever they went, whether in workhouses, hospitals, or jails, where human arrogance had not closed the door, the ghost left its blessing, imparting crucial lessons of kindness, compassion, and charity to Rutherford.

The night seemed long, yet compressed, as if the essence of the Christmas holidays was distilled into the moments they shared. Despite Rutherford's noticeable change, the ghost's demeanor turned quietly dismayed.

"Do ghosts have fleeting lives?" Rutherford inquired.

"My time on Earth is fleeting indeed," replied the ghost. "It ends tonight."

"Tonight!" Rutherford exclaimed.

"Yes, at midnight. Listen! The time draws near."

As the chimes struck a quarter past eleven, Rutherford noticed something peculiar protruding from beneath the ghost's robe. "Forgive my curiosity, but what is that peeking out—a foot or a claw?" he asked.

"With the flesh upon it, it may well be a claw," the ghost replied, revealing two children hidden beneath its garment. They were wretched, miserable, and frightful, clinging to the ghost's robe. "Look here, man! Look down!" the ghost exclaimed. The children appeared sickly, thin, ragged, and filled with anger. Demons glared menacingly from where angels should have sat enthroned. No degradation or perversion of humanity could match the horror of these poor, forsaken children.

Rutherford was shocked and tried to say that they were fine children, but the words choked themselves, rather than be parties to a lie of such enormous magnitude. "Ghost, are they your children?" Rutherford could say no more.

"They belong to all of mankind," the ghost replied, gazing down at them. "He is Ignorance. She is Want. Beware them both, but especially the boy, for I see doom upon his brow, unless it can be erased. Deny it!" the ghost cried, pointing toward the city. "Slander those who speak the truth. Accept it for your own selfish purposes and make it worse. And suffer the consequences."

"Have they no refuge or resources?" Rutherford inquired.

"Are there no prisons?" the ghost retorted, echoing Rutherford's previous words. "Are there no workhouses?"

As a distant bell struck three, Rutherford looked around for the ghost, but it had vanished. With the last chime fading, he recalled Marley's warning to expect the last ghost when the clock struck three. Raising his eyes, Rutherford saw a solemn dark phantom approaching, drifting like a mist along the ground.

The Last Spirit

THE GHOST APPROACHED SLOWLY AND silently, creating an atmosphere of gloom and mystery. It was dressed in a black garment that covered its head, face, and body, with only one outstretched hand visible. The presence of the ghost filled Rutherford with solemn dread, and although it didn't speak or move, he felt its tall and imposing nature. Rutherford asked if the apparition was the Ghost of Christmas Yet to Come, to which the ghost only pointed down.

Rutherford understood that the ghost would show him future events that were yet to happen. Despite being accustomed to the company of ghosts, his legs trembled, and he struggled to stand upright. The ghost paused briefly, noticing Rutherford's condition, and gave him time to recover. But this only made Rutherford feel more frightened, knowing that behind the dark shroud were ghostly eyes fixed on him. Although he strained his eyes to see, all he could make out was the uncanny hand and a large black hooded figure. Rutherford expressed his fear of the ghost of the future but acknowledged that he believed its purpose was to bring him good. He was willing to accompany the ghost and do so with a grateful heart. However, the ghost remained silent, pointing straight ahead with its hand.

Rutherford urged the ghost to lead the way. He followed in the shadow of the ghost's garment, feeling supported and carried along by it. As they moved, it seemed as if the city had sprung up around them, enveloping them in its bustling activity. They found themselves at the Boston courthouse, amid lawyers scurrying about, jingling coins in their pockets, conversing in groups, and checking their watches, just as Rutherford had seen them do so many times before.

The ghost stopped beside a group of lawyers, and seeing that the hand was pointing at them, Rutherford moved closer to listen to their conversation.

"I don't know much about it," said a stout man with a large chin. "All I know is that he's dead."

"When did he die?" another person asked.

"Last night, I believe," someone replied.

"What was the cause of his death?" a third person asked, taking a casual puff on a cigar.

"I have no idea," the first person replied with a yawn.

"What did he do with his money?" asked a red-faced gentleman with a drooping nose. "I haven't heard anything about it."

"He probably left it to his law firm," the man with the large chin replied, yawning again. "He didn't leave it to me. That's for sure." This remark was met with a general laugh.

"It seems like it will be a very modest funeral," the same person said. "I don't know anyone who will attend. Shall we organize a party and volunteer?"

"I don't mind going if there's food," the man with the drooping nose remarked. "But I need to be fed if I'm going to attend."

"Well, I'm the most selfless among you," the first speaker said. "I never wear black, and I never eat lunch. But I'll offer to go if someone else does. Actually, now that I think about it, I might have been his closest friend. We used to stop and talk whenever we saw each other at the courthouse."

The speakers and listeners dispersed and joined other groups. Rutherford recognized these men and looked to the ghost for an explanation. The ghost glided into a street and pointed its finger at two people who were meeting. Rutherford listened, hoping to find an explanation there. He knew these men very well. They were successful lawyers, wealthy and influential. Rutherford always made sure to maintain a good relationship with them, strictly from a business perspective.

"How are you?" one of them greeted.

"Very well… and you?" the other replied.

"Well," said the first. "Old Scratch has finally gotten what he deserved, huh?"

"That's what I heard," the second responded. "It's cold, isn't it?"

"Normal for Christmas time."

"Yes, I suppose," he answered casually. "It was nice to see you. Have a good morning."

They didn't exchange anything else. That was their meeting: conversation and farewell. Rutherford found it surprising that the ghost attached importance to such seemingly insignificant conversations. He couldn't imagine how these conversations related to the death of his old partner, Edward Marley, because that was in the past, and the ghost's domain was the future. He also couldn't think of anyone connected to him who would be relevant. But he was confident that whoever these conversations applied to, they held a moral lesson for his own improvement.

Rutherford resolved to remember every word he heard and everything he saw, especially when it involved his own shadow. He expected that observing his future self's actions would provide the missing clue and make solving these mysteries easier. Rutherford looked around, hoping to see his own reflection in that very place. However, another man stood in Rutherford's usual spot at the courthouse.

They left the courthouse and entered a part of Boston that Rutherford had never been to before, though he recognized its location and bad reputation. The streets were dirty and narrow, the shops and houses shabby, and the people poorly dressed, drunk, and careless. The alleys and archways served as cesspools, emitting foul smells, dirt, and the misery of life.

In the depths of this infamous street, there was a shop beneath a decrepit roof, where they bought iron, old rags, and bottles. Inside, heaps of rusty keys, nails, chains, hinges, files, and other various discarded pieces of iron were piled on the floor. Secrets that few would want to investigate were hidden among mountains of unsightly rags, filth, and stacks of garbage. Sitting amid the goods was a gray-haired thieving scoundrel, almost seventy years old. His name was Dan—old Dan, to those who knew him. He was bald, and had the expression of a dullard, who had been kicked in the head by a donkey. Old Dan kept himself protected from the cold air outside with a tattered curtain made of various tattered clothes hanging on a line.

Rutherford and the ghost encountered this person just as a wretched old woman with a heavy bundle entered the shop. But before she could settle in, another woman with a similar load also arrived, closely followed by a man in faded black. The people entering the shop jolted in surprise at seeing each other, and after a moment of astonishment, old Dan joined in their laughter.

"Let Caroline Zito, the cleaning lady, go first!" exclaimed Debora Carson, who had entered the room with the first bundle. "Let me go second and let Roger, the undertaker's assistant, go third. This is quite a coincidence, Dan. We all met here at the same time for the same purpose without planning it!"

Caroline Zito was a wretched old sinner, with a malevolent aura casting a shadow of darkness over all who encountered her. With a wrinkled face that was covered with warts, and eyes smoldering with malice, she was a haunting figure that embodied the very essence of a mean-spirited and bitter old hag.

"You couldn't have met in a better place," said old Dan, taking his pipe out of his mouth. "Come into the living room. You're all welcome here. But wait until I close the shop door. Come into the living room. Come in!"

The living room was the area behind the rag curtain. Old Dan stoked the flames in the fireplace with an old curtain rod, and lit his oil lamp, as it was nighttime, using the stem of his pipe. While he did this, Debora, who had already spoken, threw her bundle on the floor and sat down boldly on a stool, crossing her arms while looking defiantly at the other two.

"What does it matter?" said Debora. "Every person has a right to take care of themselves. *He* always did."

"That's true, indeed," said Caroline. "No man more so. We've done nothing wrong, taking what we could!"

"Very well, then!" cried Debora. "Who is worse off because of the loss of a few things like these? Certainly not a dead man, I suppose."

"I would agree," said Caroline, cackling. "If he wanted to keep them after he was dead, that greedy old miser, why wasn't he generous in his lifetime? If he had been, he would have had someone to take care of him when he was struck by death, instead of lying there, gasping out his last breath, all alone."

"It's the truest words ever spoken," said Debora. "It's a punishment for him."

"I wish it was a heavier punishment," replied Caroline. "And it would have been, you can depend on it, if I could have found anything else. Open that bundle, old Dan, and let me know the value of it. Speak plainly. I'm not afraid to be the first or for them to see it. We pretty well know that we were helping each other before we met here. It's not a sin. Open the bundle, Dan."

But the undertaker's assistant, stepping forward and going first, showed his stolen items. It wasn't much. A few seals, a pencil case, a pair of sleeve buttons, and a brooch of little value. Each item was examined and appraised by old Dan, who wrote the amount he was willing to pay for each item on the wall.

"That's all you'll get," said Dan. "And I wouldn't give another dollar, even if I were to be boiled for not doing it. Who's next?"

Caroline was next. Sheets and towels, a few items of clothing, two old-fashioned silver teaspoons, a pair of sugar tongs, and a few pairs of boots. Her estimate was written on the wall in the same way. "I always give too much to ladies. It's a weakness of mine, and that's how I ruin myself," said old Dan. "That's all you'll get. If you asked me for another penny, I would regret being so generous and knock off a dollar."

"And now, Dan, open my bundle," said Debora. Dan knelt down to open it more easily, and after untying many knots, he pulled out a large and heavy roll of dark material.

"What do you call this?" asked Dan. "Bed curtains?"

"Yes," Debora replied, laughing, and leaning forward on her crossed arms. "Bed curtains."

"You don't mean to say you took them down, rings and all, while he was lying there?" said Dan.

"Yes, I do," she answered. "Why not?"

"You were destined to make your fortune by your evil nature," said Dan, "and you certainly will."

"I won't hold back when I can get something by reaching out for it, especially not for a man like him. I promise you, Dan," she said calmly. "Be careful not to spill oil on the blankets."

"Whose blankets?" Dan asked.

"Whose do you think?" she replied. "He's not likely to catch a cold without them, I dare say."

"I hope he didn't die of something contagious, eh?" old Dan said, pausing in his work and looking up.

"Don't worry about that," Debora assured him. "I'm not so fond of his company that I would stick around for something like that if he did. Ah, you can search through that shirt until your eyes ache, but you won't find a hole or worn-out spot. It was the best he had, and a fine one at that. They would have wasted it if it weren't for me."

"What do you mean by wasting it?" old Dan asked.

"Putting it on him to be buried in, of course," Debora said with a sinister laugh. "Someone was foolish enough to do it, but I took it off again. If calico isn't good enough for that purpose, then it's not good enough for anything. It's just as fitting for the body. He can't look any worse than he did in that shirt."

Rutherford listened to this conversation in horror. As they sat gathered around their stolen goods, illuminated by the dim light of the old man's lamp, he viewed them with detestation and disgust, as if they were demons selling the corpse itself.

"Ha, ha!" Caroline laughed when old Dan, producing a bag of money, counted out their individual gains on the ground. "This is the result, you see. He scared everyone away from him when he was alive, only to benefit us when he was dead. Ha, ha, ha!"

"Ghost," Rutherford said, shuddering from head to foot. "I see that the fate of this unfortunate man could be my own. My life is heading in that direction now. Merciful Heaven, what is this?"

Suddenly, the scene had changed, and now he was standing at the side of a bed—a bare, uncovered bed. Beneath a ragged sheet, there lay something covered up. The room was too dark to be observed accurately, although Rutherford glanced around in response to an inner impulse, eager to know what kind of room it was.

A pale light from outside fell directly on the bed, and on it, robbed and abandoned, neglected and uncared for, lay the body of a man. Rutherford looked toward the ghost, as its steady hand pointed to the body. The cover was so carelessly arranged that the slightest movement—the motion of a finger from Rutherford—would have revealed the face. He thought about it, felt how easy it would be to do it, and longed to do it, but he had no more power to lift the veil than to dismiss the ghost at his side.

Rutherford wondered what this man would have been thinking if he were alive. Greed, dishonesty, and a burning desire for money. These are the things that led him to this unfortunate end. He lay in the dark, empty house with no one to say that he was ever kind to them. A cat scratched at the door, and there were rats gnawing beneath the floor. Rutherford didn't want to think about why they were in the room of death or why they seemed so restless and disturbed.

"Ghost," he said. "This is a terrifying place. Even when I leave, I won't forget the lesson it has taught me. Let's go."

But the ghost continued to point to the body.

"I understand," Rutherford replied, "and I would look. But I don't have the power, Ghost. I don't have the strength."

The ghost seemed to look at him again.

"If there's anyone in town who feels any emotion because of this man's death," Rutherford pleaded, "show that person to me, Ghost, I beg you."

* * *

The ghost briefly spread its dark robe like a wing, and then revealed a room in daylight. A mother and her children were in the room. She was waiting for someone with anxious eagerness. She paced back and forth, startled at every sound, looked out the window, glanced at the clock, tried to work with her needle but couldn't concentrate, and could hardly bear the voices of the children playing. Finally, they heard the long-awaited knock. She hurried to the door and met her husband, a young man with a tired and sad face. He sat down for the dinner that had been kept warm for him by the fire. When she asked if there was any news, after a long silence, he seemed unsure how to answer.

"Is it good?" she asked, trying to help him.

"Bad," he replied. "We're completely ruined."

"No. There's still hope, Howard."

The man shook his head ruefully.

"If he changes his mind," she said, "then there is hope. Nothing is beyond hope if such a miracle were to happen."

"He won't change his wretched mind," her husband said. "He's dead."

If her face told the truth, she was a gentle, loving woman, but grateful to hear the news of this death, and laughed. But she quickly clasped her hands together, and then asked for forgiveness and apologized for her initial reaction. Her first response came from the depth of her heart. "What the half-drunk old woman, Mrs. Carson, told me last night, when I tried to see him and asked for a week's extension on the loan, turned out to be true. He wasn't just very ill. He was dying." She paused. "Who will we owe the debt to now?"

"I don't know. But by the time that happens, we'll have the money ready. And even if we don't, it would be a terrible fate to have yet another merciless lawyer as his successor. Tonight, we can sleep with light hearts, dearest," he said.

Without even trying, their hearts were lighter being with each other. The house was happier because of this man's death. The only emotion that the ghost could show Rutherford in response to this event was one of pleasure.

"Show me some tenderness connected with a death," Rutherford said. "There must be something resembling a warm feeling. Show it to me!"

* * *

The ghost led him through several familiar streets, but Rutherford couldn't spot himself anywhere. They entered poor William Cratchit's house, the same one Rutherford had visited before, and found the mother and children sitting around the fire.

Everything was quiet. So very quiet. The little Cratchits were sitting still in one corner, looking up at Peter, who had a book in front of him. The mother and her daughters were sewing, but did not speak.

Mrs. Cratchit placed her work on the table and covered her face with her hand. "The color hurts my eyes," she said. "They're better now. The candlelight weakens them, and I wouldn't want to show watery eyes to your father when he comes home. It must be close to his time."

"Actually, past his time," Peter replied, closing his book. "But I think he's been walking a little slower than usual these past few evenings, Mother."

They fell silent again. Finally, she spoke in a steady and cheerful voice, though it faltered once: "I have seen him walk with Tiny Tim on his shoulders, very fast indeed."

"And so have I," cried Peter. "Often."

"And so have I," exclaimed another. Everyone had.

"But Tiny Tim was very light to carry," she continued, focused on her work. "And his father loved him so much that it was no trouble—no trouble at all." Mrs. Cratchit heard the front door open. "And there's your father now!"

Mrs. Cratchit rushed out to meet him, and William, bundled up in his scarf, entered. His tea was waiting for him on the stove, and everyone competed to help William with his coat and to bring him a warm drink.

When William sat down by the fireplace, the two young Cratchits climbed onto his knees and pressed their little cheeks against his face, as if to say, "Don't worry, Father. Don't be sad."

William was cheerful with them and spoke kindly to the whole family. He looked at the work on the table and praised Mrs. Cratchit and the girls for their hard work with sewing a new blanket.

"Did you go today?" his wife asked.

"Yes, my dear," he replied.

"I wish you could have gone. It would have been good for you to see how green it is there at the cemetery. But you'll see it often. I promised little Tim that we would go there every Sunday to visit." William suddenly broke down and cried. He couldn't help it. "My sweet little Tim!" William wept. "My dear little boy!"

They gathered around the fire, and William told them about the incredible kindness of Mr. Rutherford's niece—Julia. They had bumped into each other on the street that day, and when Julia saw that William looked a little down, she asked what was troubling him. William told her about the death of Tiny Tim.

"Julia is the most pleasant-spoken lady you'll ever meet," said William. "'I am sincerely sorry, Mr. Cratchit, and truly sorry for your dear wife.' That's what Juila said to me." He paused to smile. "I have no idea how she knew that?"

"Knew what, my dear?"

"Why, that you are a good wife," William replied.

"Everyone knows that," Peter chimed in.

"Very well said, my boy!" William exclaimed. "I hope they do. 'Sincerely sorry,' Julia said, 'for your good wife. If there's anything I can do to help you,' she said, giving me her card. 'That's where I live. Please come to me.'" William cried, "Just for the sake of what she might be able to do for us, but more for her kind manner. It truly felt like she had known our Tiny Tim and sympathized with us."

"I'm sure she's a good person," Mrs. Cratchit said.

"You would be certain of it, my dear," William replied. "If you saw and spoke to her. And she offered to get Peter a better job. I wouldn't be surprised if she did so."

"Just listen to that, Peter," Mrs. Cratchit said.

"And then," one of the girls cried, "Peter will find a wife and live on his own."

"Come on, get out of here!" Peter retorted, grinning.

"It's just as likely as not," William said. "One of these days, though there's plenty of time for that, my dear. But no matter when and how we part from each other, I'm sure we won't forget poor Tiny Tim—will we—or this first parting that we had among us."

"Never, Father!" they all cried.

"And I know," William said, "I know, my dears, that when we remember how patient and kind he was, even though he was a little child, we won't easily argue with each other and forget about poor Tiny Tim."

"No, never, Father!" they all cried again.

"That makes me happy," William said. "I love you all so much!"

Mrs. Cratchit kissed William, and said, "Oh! Tiny Tim, his little soul is now with God."

* * *

The Ghost of Christmas Yet to Come led him into the business district near his law firm. The ghost didn't stop for anything, but walked straight on without hesitation, until Rutherford begged him to wait for a moment.

"This street," Rutherford said, "is where my office is, and has been since it first opened. I see the building. I want to see what I'll become in the future." Rutherford hurried to the window of his office and looked in. It was still an office, but not his. The furniture was different, and the person in the chair wasn't him. He was about to speak, when suddenly, the city vanished.

In the blink of an eye, Rutherford and the ghost now stood on a creaking dock at the shoreline of a desolate fishing port, amid the approach of a fierce storm. The air was thick with the briny scent of the ocean, and the taste of salt lingered on Rutherford's lips. Above, the sky was a canvas of swirling dark clouds, illuminated by the occasional crackling of lightning. The silence was eerie, broken only by the distant rumble of thunder, which echoed like a foreboding drumroll. Rutherford was bound in heavy chains that were attached to an iron money safe. He stood at the edge of the dock, his heart pounding as he looked out at the tumultuous sea. The waves crashed against the wooden pillars, sending icy spray into the air. Each droplet felt like a tiny needle piercing his skin, adding to the chilling atmosphere. With the chains that clung tightly to Rutherford's body, he stood before the ghost as it pointed down to the icy waters of the Atlantic—the same that consumed Edward Marley.

As the thunder roared overhead, Rutherford's hands strained against the iron shackles, but they held firm. The ghost pointed from the dark ocean to him and then back again.

"No, Ghost! Oh no, no!" The finger was still pointing to the ocean. "Ghost!" he cried, grabbing onto its robe. "Listen to me. I am not the same man I used to be. I won't become the man I would have been without this experience. Why show me this if there is no hope for me?"

For the first time, the hand of the ghost seemed to shake angrily, still pointing insistently at the icy water.

"Good Spirit," he continued, falling to his knees on the dock before the ghost. "People's actions will predict certain outcomes, which, if unchanged, will lead to this end," Rutherford said. "But if the actions change, the end result *will* change. Tell me I can still change the future you have shown me by living a different life."

The ghostly hand trembled, still pointing to the ocean.

"I will celebrate Christmas in my heart and try to keep that spirit all year round. I will live in the past, present, and future. The lessons that the ghosts have taught me will not be ignored. Oh, tell me this is not my fate. Mercy! Show me mercy! I am not the same man."

In despair, he grabbed the ghost by the hand. It struggled to break free, but Rutherford held on tightly. The ghost, even stronger, pushed him away. Raising his hands in a final prayer to have his fate reversed, he saw a change in the ghost's hood and clothing. It shrank, collapsed, and transformed into a bedpost in Rutherford's house.

STAVE V

The End of It

Yᴇs! Aɴᴅ ʙᴇʜᴏʟᴅ, ᴛʜᴇ ʙᴇᴅᴘᴏsᴛ belonged to him. The bed was his, as was everything in the room. But the most incredible thing of all was that the time yet to come, the future, was his to mend!

"I shall live in the past, the present, and the future!" Rutherford exclaimed as he leaped from his bed. "The ghosts of all three shall live within me. Oh, Edward Marley! Let heaven and the spirit of Christmas be praised for this! I say it with humility, old Edward. I say it with all of my heart!"

He was so overwhelmed with emotion and determination that his words, cracked and broken, could barely find their way out. He had wept profusely during his encounter with the Ghost of Christmas Future, and his face was still damp with tears.

"They were not stolen!" cried Rutherford, clutching one of his bed curtains tightly. "They are here, I am here, and the specters of what could have been shall be banished. I know it! I feel it!"

As he rushed with excitement to his wardrobe and attempted to put on an outfit, he turned his clothes inside out, put them on upside down, tore them, and misplaced them. "I don't know what to do!" exclaimed Rutherford, laughing. "I am as light as a feather, as joyful as an angel, as merry as a schoolboy. I am as giddy as a drunken man. A merry Christmas to all! Happy New Year to the entire world. Hooray! Hallelujah!"

Rutherford ran into the sitting room, his excitement leaving him breathless. "There's the old chair by the fireplace!" he exclaimed, starting off again and joyfully hopping around the wooden floor. "There's the door through which the ghost of Edward Marley entered. There's the corner where the Ghost of Christmas Present stood! It's all real, all true; it all happened. Ha, ha!"

Truly, for a man who had not laughed in so many years, it was a magnificent laugh—a truly remarkable one. The beginning of a long series of glorious laughter!

"I don't know what day of the month it is!" said Rutherford. "I don't know how long I've been with the ghosts. I know nothing. I feel like a child. But it doesn't matter. I don't care. I'd rather be a child. Hooray! I'm alive and have been given a second chance!"

His excitement was interrupted by the sound of the church bells ringing the most delightful chimes he had ever heard. Clash, clang, hammer, ding, dong, bell. Running to the window, he opened it and stuck his head out. No fog nor mist greeted him; it was beautifully clear, bright, and cheerful—invigorating and cold enough to make the blood dance. Golden sunlight; heavenly blue sky; fresh, sweet air. Oh, magnificent!

"What day is it?" cried Rutherford, calling down to a small boy in Sunday clothes who was walking on the street below his window.

"Huh?" replied the boy with a look of wonder.

"What day is it, my fine young fellow?" said Rutherford.

"Today?" answered the boy. "Why, it's Christmas day."

"It's Christmas Day!" said Rutherford to himself. *I didn't miss it. The ghosts did everything in one night. They can do whatever they want. Of course they can...* "Hello, young lad!"

"Hello!" replied the boy.

"Do you know the poultry shop in the street just past the next one on the corner?" Rutherford asked.

"I should hope so," replied the boy.

"An intelligent boy!" said Rutherford. "An impressive child! Do you know if they've sold the big turkey that was hanging there?"

"You mean the one as big as me?" returned the boy.

"What a delightful boy!" said Rutherford. "It's a pleasure to talk to you. Yes, my friend!"

"It's still hanging there," replied the boy.

"Is it?" said Rutherford. "Well... go and buy it."

"Seriously?"

"Yes, yes," said Rutherford. "I mean it. Buy it and tell them to bring it here so that I can give them the address of where to take it. Come back with the man, and I'll give you five dollars. Come back with him in less than five minutes, and I'll give you ten!"

The boy ran off as fast as a bullet.

"I'll send it to William Cratchit's!" whispered Rutherford, rubbing his hands together briskly and laughing. "He won't know who sent it. It's twice the size of Tiny Tim!"

His hand shook as he wrote the address, but he somehow scribbled it down. Then, he went downstairs to open the front door, ready for the arrival of the Poulterer's man.

It was a magnificent turkey! "Well, it's impossible to carry that to the Cratchit's home," said Rutherford. "You'll need a cab." Rutherford paid to have it delivered in a taxi.

Shaving was not a simple task, as his hand continued to shake with excitement. But if he had cut off the end of his nose, he wouldn't care.

Rutherford dressed himself in his best clothes and finally went out into the streets. The people were now pouring out of their homes and churches, just as he had seen them with the Ghost of Christmas Present. Walking with his hands behind him, Rutherford looked at everyone with a joyful smile. In fact, he looked so incredibly pleasant that three or four good-natured passersby said, "Good morning, sir! Merry Christmas to you!" Rutherford often said afterward that of all the cheerful sounds he had ever heard, those salutations were the most cheerful ones.

He hadn't gone far when he saw two gentlemen coming toward him—the same gentlemen who had walked into his office the day before and said, "Rutherford and Marley's, I presume?" It pained him to think about how these old gentlemen would look at him when they met, but he knew the path he had to take.

"My dear sirs," said Rutherford, quickening his pace and taking the old gentlemen by both hands. "How are you? Merry Christmas to you both!"

"Mr. Rutherford?" one of them asked, looking at him strangely.

"Yes," said Rutherford. "That's my name, and I'm afraid it may not be pleasant for you. Allow me to apologize. I wish to donate, and will you please accept—" Rutherford's voice dropped as he whispered in their ears.

"Good heavens!" exclaimed one of the gentlemen, as if he had lost his breath. "Dear Mr. Rutherford, are you serious?"

"If you please," said Rutherford. "Not a penny less. There are many back payments included, I assure you. Will you do me that favor?"

"My dear sir," said the other, briskly shaking hands with him. "I don't know what to say to such generosity—"

"Don't say anything, please," replied Rutherford. "Will you come and visit me?"

"I will!" exclaimed the old gentleman. And it was clear that he intended to follow through.

"Thank you," said Rutherford. "I am very grateful. Thank you. Bless you!"

Rutherford walked past a church, strolled through the bustling streets, observed the hurried passersby, tenderly tousled the heads of children, stole glances into the cozy kitchens of houses, and cast his gaze upward to the windows. To his astonishment, he discovered that every little thing had the power to fill him with joy. Never before had he imagined that a simple walk or any other ordinary activity could bring him such boundless happiness. As the afternoon unfolded, he made his way toward his niece's apartment.

He circled the door several times, gathering the courage to ascend the steps and knock. With resolve in his heart, he finally took the plunge. "Is Julia home, my dear?" Rutherford inquired of a young girl who answered the door.

"Yes, sir," the woman replied.

"Where can I find her, my dear?" Rutherford pressed further.

"She's in the dining room, sir, with her friend. I can show you the way upstairs, if you please."

"Thank you, dear."

When they reached her apartment, he gently turned the handle and peered into the room. Julia and her friend were engrossed in conversation by the fireplace and the beautifully decorated Christmas tree.

"Julia!" Rutherford called out from outside her door.

"Well, bless my soul!" Julia exclaimed, eyes widened. "Who's there?"

"It's me, your Uncle Henry. I've come for dinner. Will you let me in, Julia?"

She embraced him with all her might. It was the warmest reception one could hope for. For the first time, they sat down together as a family, sharing a meal. It was the most precious gift Rutherford could have given to Julia. Finally, they were united as a family.

* * *

Rutherford was early at the office the next morning. If only he could be there first and catch William Cratchit arriving late! And he did—yes, he did! The clock struck nine. No sign of William. A quarter past. Still no William. He was a full eighteen and a half minutes late. Rutherford sat with his door wide open, hoping to catch a glimpse of him entering the office.

William took off his hat and scarf before opening the door. He quickly sat on his stool and started working with his pen, as if trying to catch up.

"Hey!" grumbled Rutherford, pretending to be annoyed. "What do you think you're doing coming in at this hour?"

"I'm very sorry, Mr. Rutherford," said William. "I'm running late."

"You are?" said Rutherford. "Yes, I think you are. Come this way, please."

"It's only once a year, Sir," pleaded William, timidly stepping into his office. "It won't happen again. I was celebrating a bit too much yesterday."

"Now, listen here, my friend," said Rutherford, standing up and giving William a playful jab in the chest that made him stumble back. "I can't tolerate this anymore. And because of that," he continued, "I have no other choice but to triple your salary and add a bonus as well!"

William cocked his head, eyes narrowed. "Sir?" was all he could mutter.

"A Merry Christmas, William!" said Rutherford with an unmistakable sincerity as he patted him on the back. "A happier Christmas, William, my good friend, than I have given you in many years! I will triple your salary and help your struggling family. We will discuss your future this afternoon over lunch. Make sure to stoke the fires and buy more coal before you begin your work, William!"

Rutherford kept his word and did all of that, and even more. And to Tiny Tim, who did *not* die, Rutherford was like a second father. He became a good friend to the people of Boston, an honest attorney, and a caring man. Some people laughed at the change in him, but he didn't pay them much attention. He knew that whenever something good happened, there would always be people who found reasons to laugh at it. And he believed it was better for them to laugh than to be bitter. He felt nothing but love in his heart, and that was enough for him.

He never heard from the ghosts again, and lived his life with kindness, mercy, and charity. It was always said of him that he knew how to celebrate Christmas well, and if anyone possessed the knowledge to do so, it was Henry Rutherford.

May the same be said of all of us! And so, as Tiny Tim observed, "God bless us—everyone!"

THE END